Peter and Friends
At Camp

By
Rosanna Scott

Illustrated by
Todd Fargo

Jason and Nordic Publishers
Hollidaysburg, Pennsylvania

ARTHRITIS FOUNDATION® Take Control. We Can Help.™

A Word About The Arthritis Foundation

The Arthritis Foundation is committed to serving the special needs of children, teens and young adults with juvenile arthritis through special programs, such as support groups, camps and its annual national conference for families. The Arthritis Foundation also serves as a clearinghouse of information for families through its Web site, brochures, books and its bimonthly newsletter *Kids Get Arthritis Too.*

For more information or to find a chapter near you,
call 800-568-4045 or visit **www.arthritis.org.**

****

For additional titles of **Turtle Books** *for children with special needs and their friends*
please visit:
www.jasonandnordic .com

Peter and Friends at Camp

Text and Illustration copyright © 2006 Jason & Nordic Publishers

Library of Congress Cataloging in Publication Data

Library of Congress Cataloging-in-Publication Data

Scott, Rosanna, 1969-
  Peter and friends at camp / by Rosanna Scott ; illustrated by Todd Fargo.
    p. cm.
  Summary: Eight-year-old Peter, who has juvenile rheumatoid arthritis, is worried when he goes to camp for the first time, but because he and his buddy, Dalton, who has cerebral palsy, stick together, Peter is even able to face his fear of swimming.
  ISBN 0-944727-52-2 (lib. bdg. : alk. paper) -- ISBN 0-944727-51-4 (pbk. : alk. paper)
  [1. Camps--Fiction. 2. People with disabilities--Fiction. 3. Friendship--Fiction.
4. Courage--Fiction.] I. Fargo, Todd, 1963- ill. II. Title.
  PZ7.S4287Pet 2006
  [E]--dc22

                                        2006041831

ISBN 0-944727-51-4 paper edition
ISBN 0-944727-52-2 library edition

Printed in the U.S.A.
On acid free paper

To Craig,

My hero

and to

Mitchell
and
Deavan,

the lights of my life

Peter watched trees whiz by the car windows. "How much farther to Camp Courage?" he asked.

"What's Camp Courage?" asked Curtis for the hundredth time.

"It's a fun camp for kids like Peter," Mom answered.

"So it's for kids who have arth-ur-i-t-is, right?"

"It's arthritis, Curtis and it's for kids like me," Peter said.

"How did you catch it?"

"Not that again! Mom tell him I didn't catch it," Peter yelled.

"Curtis, we've told you before. You can't catch arthritis. When Peter was six, he started having a lot of pain in his arms and legs. Then his joints started swelling and turning red. When we took him to the doctor, they ran tests and found out that he has..."

"I know! JRA for short! Does that mean I'm going to catch it when I'm six?" Curtis asked.

"No, Curtis. Just because Peter has it, doesn't mean you'll get it."

"OK. But, why does Grandpa use a cane? When we went fishing he said he has arth-ur-i-tis? Grandpa is old and he has JRA!"

"That's not JRA! Kids get JRA. If you're older, it's not JRA it's just arthritis!" Peter said.

"That's right, Peter." Mom answered.

"OK!" Curtis said. "Aren't we there yet?"

Peter closed his eyes and took a deep breath. He began to worry about swimming. How will I do in the water, he wondered. I get so scared in the water. They said they do the water stuff a lot. I know I can't do it. If the kids find out they'll think I'm a scaredy-cat or something!

Before he could think anymore, Dad called, "We're here. Ready to make some new friends, Peter?"

Dad pulled into the campground and drove up to a big building.

"Wow! Cool!" Curtis said. "Can I stay, too?"

"No, Curtis!" Mom said. "You'll go to camp someday, but not today!"

As Dad took Peter's suitcases out of the trunk, a lady walked towards them.

"Hi there, I'm Miss Amy,"

"Hi, I'm Peter," Peter said shyly.

"This is Dalton," she said. Peter saw a small red-haired boy with a walker peeking around her.

"Hey, Peter," Dalton said.

"You and Dalton are going to be camp buddies this week. By the end of the week you should be great friends."

Peter, Curtis, Mom and Dad went to Peter's room and helped put his things away. After Peter and Dalton were unpacked, all the kids and parents met at the campfire circle.

A man played a bugle, the flags were raised and Camp Courage had begun. Counselors talked about what the campers would be doing all week.

Parents got to ask questions. Then it was time for the parents to go home.

Mom, Dad and even Curtis hugged Peter.

"Don't worry about the water," Mom said. "You'll do just fine."

"OK, Mom," Peter answered. He wished he could feel better about it. After his mom and dad left, the counselors led their groups back to the rooms.

Back in the room, Dalton was very quiet. He looked like he was going to cry.

"Dalton, are you OK?" Peter asked. Dalton just shrugged his shoulders. "What's wrong?"

Dalton looked at Peter and said, "I've got cerebral palsy and need help with clothes and things. I guess I'm scared. I've never been away from home before."

"Neither have I," said Peter. "So let's help each other, OK?"

Dalton looked at Peter for a second and then said, "OK! We stick together!"

They did stick together. They helped each
other at the craft cabin when they got to make
macaroni necklaces and kites.

18

They helped each other when they made
water bottle rockets and got to shoot them off.

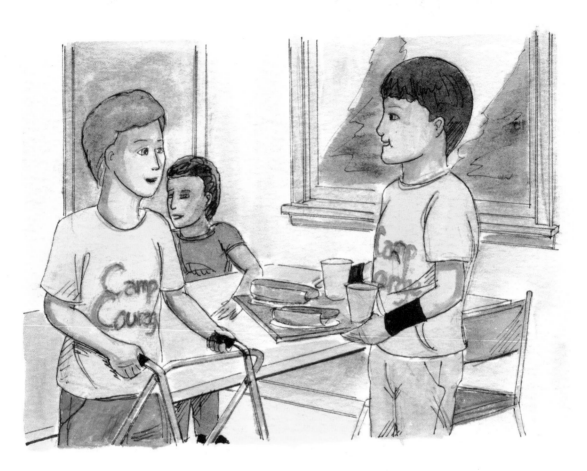

They helped each other when it was time to go to the cafeteria for their meals. They helped each other when it was time to clean up their room and do the camp chores.

No matter what they were doing, Peter and Dalton stuck together.

But then there was swimming! Peter changed into his swimming suit along with the other kids. He didn't want them to know he was afraid of the water.

Dalton put his foot in the water. "Wow, the water is cold," he said.

"It's too cold for me," Peter said.

"It'll warm up really fast once we're in," Dalton said. He used the stairs and carefully lowered himself into the water. "See, it's not so bad. Get in."

Mr. Dan, the swimming teacher came over. "How are you doing, Peter?".

"OK, Mr. Dan, but I'm not ready to go in."

"You may sit out for a few minutes then." Mr. Dan said. "When we're all in the water, we'll do some easy warm-ups," he told the group. As soon as Jill, a little girl in a wheelchair, was helped into the water they got started. They all began moving around doing their exercises... everyone except Peter.

"C'mon Peter. Get in," Dalton yelled.

Peter could tell Dalton was upset, but he shook his head 'no'.

"I don't like water very much," he answered.

"But what if we stick together? That's what you told me, right?"

Peter looked at Dalton. Dalton was right. They had planned to stick together. Peter put his big toe in the water.

"Are you ready to try, Peter?"

Peter nodded. "I'll try," he said. Slowly he walked into the water. Everyone started cheering and clapping for Peter. Peter was surprised. They didn't think he was a scaredy-cat. They wanted to help him.

"This isn't so bad." Dalton said as he splashed Peter.

"Not bad!" Peter answered and splashed him back."

The week went very fast and soon it was time for the last campfire.

"My marshmallow is on fire," one boy yelled. Miss Amy laughed and blew it out.

"I want two on my stick," Peter said.

"What about you, Dalton? How many are you going to eat?" she asked.

"I'm going to have two, just like Peter."

After they sang some camp songs, Miss Amy asked each of them to tell what they liked best about camp.

"I liked all the stuff we got to do this week," Peter said. "And...I learned I don't have to be afraid of the water."

When it was Dalton's turn, he told the group, "I liked camp because of Peter. We were best friends."

The camp fire burned low.

"Once upon a cold, dark night," Miss Amy began their last scary story. She had saved the scariest for last. They were all sure there were eyes peeking at them from the woods.

"Oh, no! I just heard something," Jill said.

"Me, too." Dalton answered.

"No," Mr. Dan said. "That's just an owl telling us it's time for bed. We pack up in the morning and you get to see your moms and dads after breakfast."

After breakfast campers and backpacks were ready. Soon cars with moms and dads filled the yard.

"Peter!" yelled Curtis, running up to Peter. "I really missed you!"

"I missed you, too," said Peter.

"Hey, Peter!" Dalton waved as he got into his car. "So long, friend!" he called.

"See you next year," Peter answered and climbed into the car beside Curtis. He showed Curtis some things he had made. He told them all about how he and Dalton helped each other and how everybody cheered for him when he got into the water.

"And guess what! I'm not afraid of water anymore," he said.

"Peter, will you show me how to do stuff and cheer for me like you and Dalton did?"

"Sure, Curtis. That's what real friends do."